I0610430

Soundings and Fathoms

stories by

Guy Biederman

Finishing Line Press
Georgetown, Kentucky

Soundings and Fathoms: Stories

"It is not down in any map; true places never are."

Herman Melville

Copyright © 2018 by Guy Biederman
ISBN 978-1-63534-670-1 First Edition
All rights reserved under International and Pan-American Copyright Conventions.
No part of this book may be reproduced in any manner whatsoever without written
permission from the publisher, except in the case of brief quotations embodied in
critical articles and reviews.

ACKNOWLEDGMENTS

Thanks to the editors of the following journals where some of these stories
first appeared.

Flash Frontier, Dreaming Backward
Carve, The Trap
Goodworks Review, Ape Man and Pink Fleece
Gathering Storm, G
Postcard Shorts, Dear Liza Dear Liza
Medusa's Laugh Press, Saturday Morning and A Story of No Consequence
daCunha, Marker 43 and Divorced Man Must Sell Bed
2 Elizabeths, Night Owl
Blue Five Notebook, Bathrobe, Biscotti, and Bike
Third Wednesday, The Most Shoplifted Poet In America
Sea Letter, Short Walk On A Long Pier
Hoot, Resume for A Guru
Exposition Review, Evan's Essence

Gratitude beyond measure to Kara for leading the charge; to my first readers:
Robert, Rosie, Tula, Chuck and Bill; to Drew and Jenn, Rex and Roy, Jim,
Dennis; to all of my students who taught me so much. In sweet memory,
Mom, Leila, Sis. And to the one who makes me possible, my one and only,
lovely Phyllis.

Publisher: Leah Maines
Editor: Christen Kincaid
Cover Art: Dennis Bayer
Author Photo: Phyllis Biederman
Cover Design: Elizabeth Maines McCleavy

Printed in the USA on acid-free paper.
Order online: www.finishinglinepress.com
                also available on amazon.com

Author inquiries and mail orders:
Finishing Line Press
P. O. Box 1626
Georgetown, Kentucky 40324
U. S. A.

Table of Contents

I have discovered
in life
that there are ways
of getting almost
anywhere you
want to go
if you really want to go.

Langston Hughes

Dreaming Backwards

I'm editing a friend's 354 page manuscript for the 9th time and still catch 67 mistakes. I'm reading it backwards to keep from understanding anything besides a typo.

Last night I dreamed backwards. You were in bed with someone else, a large and hairy but fit man. A Spanish Colonel. But I wasn't jealous or anything. He got out of bed backwards, walked backwards to the bathroom, flushed the toilet did his business, showered, put on a disheveled suit and walked backwards out of the bedroom, down the stairs—pretty impressive.

The door slammed. The car backed out of the driveway and drove down the street in reverse. It started getting lighter.

Your eyes were on me. Half hidden by the curtain, I had the feeling we were married or were going to be, but I knew someone was coming.

The thing that stayed with me was all that hair on his legs. I've never been a hairy guy. But maybe it wasn't too late.

I awoke this morning older and hairy in places I've never been. I looked at the manuscript, at its hidden typos, and retraced my steps to the bathroom, where I flushed first, feeling like I had been here before. That's the way writing has always worked for me.

The Trap

You awake to the sound of screeching and scratching and clawing and what sounds like an unruly gang just outside your bedroom window at 3 am. You slip on your sweats, grab a flashlight and the .22 and go into your backyard. Near the pond a circle of raccoons surrounds the Havahart trap that you set for whatever's been eating the lily pads and koi near the meditation bench. You figured it was maybe an opossum, skunk, or rat. You were wrong. You have an abiding hatred for raccoons—juvenile delinquents with claws who know how to open trashcans and cat doors, wreak havoc in the garden, and eat your very expensive prized koi, including Lazarus, your favorite who won't be coming back.

The circle of critters surrounding their trapped comrade scatters and retreats to the hedges of rhododendrons and azaleas and you see the bright eyes of the trapped raccoon staring back at you in the early morning moonlight.

You know what you are going to do before you do it.

You know it goes against your Buddhist teachings.

You know it's nothing you can share with Joanie—in whose dog house you've already taken up long term residence, which happens to be the guest room in the dark corner of the house with the faint smell of her sister who won't be visiting again anytime soon, still lingering within earshot of said pond.

You set the iPhone timer for four minutes and hold the trap under water. The morning goes silent, except for the garbage truck whose reverse beeping you can hear from blocks away. The animals watch you from the fence, eyes red in the dark.

You watch back. Defiant. This is your yard. Not theirs. Your territory. And this little bastard, if he lived a good life, might get lucky and come back as someone's pet cat, or maybe a guide dog, or a dolphin in the sea. Real evolution. Suburban raccoons lead a wretched existence.

Fish out of water living in these neighborhoods.

You look grimly at the submerged trap, thinking—bad pun, wondering if the surviving koi are swimming past the dead predator now, doing victory laps below the surface.

Finally the harp music sounds and you turn the timer off with your thumb and pull up the trap. It's heavier than expected. Water cascades out and you decide not to look inside. You decide you don't want this trap.

You don't want to ever do this again. Even though what you did was right. You're sure of it. Conflicted. But sure, yeah. The amount of money you save in replacement koi and lily pads alone will buy you ten more traps if it comes to that. You throw the whole mess into a triple wrapped hefty bag and walk like a Demon Santa through the dark neighborhood in your black sweats, past Volvos and lawn sprinklers and garden art from Sunset Magazine—leaving the .22 near the meditation bench—that could be awkward if you were stopped. You see the garbage truck ahead. And when the garbage man crosses the street for two cans, you heave the hefty bag into the yawning opening of the big noisy truck and walk away.

All the next day you see signs. The radio plays Rocky Raccoon. Frances, the barista at the Corner Cap, moans that she has raccoon eyes. You google raccoon. Pictures of cute little bandits, startlingly human, gaze back at you.

Over coffee you tell Syd about it. He's quiet. Doesn't finish his croissant. That evening he cancels the meditation session you both always have on Thursdays.

The next day he cancels coffee.

You think of that raccoon. You sit by the pond and meditate. The .22 sits on the rock stupa you made from Russian River Stone. A balancing act. Rusty garden art.

You think—life isn't always so simple and clear. Especially in the heat of the moment. What heat? It was three in the morning. It was in fact chilly. Cold blooded.

You realize what you are capable of. A strange awakening. Unwanted enlightenment. Your friend Syd has realized this too, apparently.

The way you both realized it about AJ when he confessed his on-going affair with the Swiss au pair and his wife Lilly never had a clue. Awkward because Lilly was a friend.

After that AJ had been uninvited to meditation.

Silently voted off Zazen Island.

We learn what we are capable of.

We learn what others can do, exceeding our expectations.

We learn how the person in front of us whom we sit zazen with, whom we share coffee with, has secrets.

You wonder how to reconcile all of this. You wonder about the word reconcile itself. How it's close in sound to raccoon. Reconcile Raccoon. Raccoonciliation.

An orange koi named Benji surfaces. Peers at you and disappears into the murky depths of the pond you haven't cleaned for weeks now.

The raccoons have not returned.

You look to the house. A curtain falls in the window of Joanie's room.

Since when did you start calling it Joanie's room?

And since when did you call yourself a Buddhist?

And Syd, your best friend?

You reach for your iPhone. See that the timer is still set on four minutes. Hit Contacts.

Take a deep breath, hold, exhale: 1-2-3-4-5.

Press AJ.

Ape Man

I put on an ape suit and walk among the living so no one will know who I am. It does not go unnoticed. Six-year-old Petey notices right away and points as his mother picks him up and they scurry away to their Town & Country mini van. The mailman grins when he hands me my stack of bills along with a flyer for heater duct cleaning in July.

I go about my day. It gets hot wearing that suit. Amazing what one gets used to. Adaptability. I go to a conference of mascots. A Giant Chicken, a Statue of Liberty, a Sumo Wrestler, and a slender French Fry with a Short Fat Sausage... I'm thinking she can do better, the Fry, but who am I to judge.

We talk about our work. Cheering teams, working crowds, holding signs for free pizza and carpet cleaning solutions, and how one day, says a Pillsbury doughboy knockoff, the people won't even notice you.

Yeah, they'll just take you for granted, says Sausage.

And that's a good thing, says Smokey.

And I can see that the room is filled with us. My tribe. I'm literally rising off my feet, walking on air three feet off the ground and the whole room looks at me.

The chant begins. *"Here we go Ape Man, here we go."*

And Rooster belts out a cock-a-doodle-do.

"Here we go Ape Man here we go!" The chant takes hold, sweeps across the room. French Fry bobs wildly. Pillsbury somersaults into Sumo who rolls him back to Panda who, in his words, *"is so damn sick of being hugged I could puke bamboo shoots."*

I am evolving backwards. I head for the door and they follow. We pour into the street, flood the sidewalks, this band of mascots, misfits, and miscreants. "Judge this," we cry with glee pinching our fur, dancing with enlightenment, or at least with the light bulbs—a set of six, multi colored who only work at Christmas but stay in their attire all year. And I see my future, as we walk across the crosswalk stopping traffic. It is nothing but authentic. A sweet rabbit walks beside me. I hold her foot with my opposable thumb. Lucky.

G

You found the letter G in your shirt pocket. 12 point. Times New Roman. Didn't think much of it until you tried to hit the __round runnin__.

Decided to stay home and fix coffee instead.

"Hey," said a nei__hbor poundin_ on the wall. "Did you hear? A letter's missin__."

Others in the complex started whinin__, too. Like a blackout or somethin__.

"Hey," said your wife __ina. "Look what happened to my name."

You fin__ered the letter in your pocket, pretended to sympathize. After all, you'd lost a first letter, too.

Your __ay brother called, said he was addin_ an e and becoming a pirate.

"Aye, aye?" You asked.

"Ar__h!" he answered.

Your mutt __uido took to the name chan__e, too. Started puttin_ on forei__n airs.

__uido?? Sounded Bushido or somethin__…

__ina moped a bit and watched __eraldo on TV. But he didn't care, his __was silent anyway. Your name on the other hand had become unpronounceable: __uy.

Ima__ine havin__ a name that even you can't say. Talk about feelin__ invisible.

People adapt to loss, or so you've been told.

The sun rose.

You tried to eschew words that used the 7th letter, but when you __limpsed the fiery sky, it slipped out. "How __lorius."

__ina, not a church __oer, murmured, " __lory be to __od."

Odd? It hit you. You weren't the only one with name issues. And if the Bi __ __uy wanted his old name back he knew where to look.

Nonchalantly, you stuffed your shirt in a ba__ and took it to __oodwill.

Acrobatease
a cocktail napkin story

"Wasn't that amazing?"
"My back hurt just watching her."
"I've never seen a stripper before."
"She wasn't a stripper, she was a topless acrobat."
"What's the difference?"
"Stripper's are more sexy."
"You didn't find her sexy?"
"Yeah, but elegant not lusty—a graceful contortionist."
"She was amazing."
"I felt weird standing around with 55 people in a Bernal Heights flat watching her contort without her shirt on."
"I thought it was artful."
"Yeah, but you were watching her poses."
"What were you watching?"
 "What most of the other guys were watching."
"Her breasts?"
"No, you."

You have a hole in your pocket. You lose stuff all the time. You name it. But stuff doesn't stay lost for long. It stays in the lining of your jacket. Big coat. Getting bigger, bulkier every year as you lose more stuff and it floats around inside. Sometimes you see the shape of lost stuff through the leather—ray bans, parker pen, a wallet with two twenties. And some hard miles, too. Each pocket has at least one hole—there are multiple entrances to the coat—like a rabbit warren for pocket stuff.

You considered asking a tailor to make repairs but then all that stuff—movie ticket, harmonica, potato peeler would be forever sewn inside and you keep hoping for the day when stuff will start falling out. For one thing, the coat's getting heavy—like those lead vests they give you in x-ray.

And sometimes, odd stuff does reappear when least expected.

Like this morning. You order a coffee and discover you'd lost yet another billfold to the lining of the coat. And the barista was giving you the eye.

Or so you thought.

"Love your coat," she said.

"Thanks."

"I covet it," she whispered, handing over your cup of pour over dark roast.

You nodded. Handed her a toothbrush that surfaced where your wallet had been. She placed the toothbrush in the register next to a pocketknife and a comb, never taking her eyes off your coat, perhaps even undressing you. You marveled at her dexterity—the way some typists tap keys without looking.

"How much for the coat?" she asked.

"You name it."

"I'm not gonna buy it. I like to look at what I can't have and let it go," she breathed. Her biceps were defined, her eyes a piercing blue.

You shivered. Left a roll of duct tape in the tip jar.

Saturday Morning

The cats don't know it's Saturday. Pontiac hops on the bed and meows to be fed, standing in the empty place where Pearl used to sleep. I open one eye and get a fix on the clock: 5:23. Way too early for a weekend. I hold out a hand. Try to mollify with a stroke of his silky head. Pontiac keeps his distance.

Jade Blue the Siamese is having her way with the carpet. I roll over and close my ears. That's when Pontiac goes to level 2 and starts licking my lobe. After four scratch pad licks I'm back on my back and the big dude goes heavy, stepping onto my chest with all fours taking away any chance I have to breathe. He knows it. I know it. It's time.

Truth is Pontiac belonged to Pearl. She'd rescued him from an ex who had been ignoring the enormous, needy Tabby. Now I was part of the ex line. Somehow Pontiac stayed behind. I get it. Pearl's a gypsy who lives on cinnamon, coffee, and cigarettes, who loves pomegranates and cats-in-need, who looks younger and more waifish by the day, with a turquoise voice that holds every cafe captive when she takes her turn at the mic.

I speak from experience.

I stagger to the kitchen and speak to Pontiac who purrs against my legs. Jade Blue waits by the window, content to let big fella work. I open a fresh can of Fancy Feast. Pontiac meows. Rises on his back legs. Jade Blue joins the party.

"I know, I miss her, too." I set the open can on the counter and take a small pleasure in making them wait just a little while longer.

And I put the coffee on.

MARKER 43

You pull on the drawer of the antique highboy of tongue and groove construction and the knob comes off in your hand. Shit. You slip the knob back on the dowel. The empty drawer stays closed. Downstairs, your husband Dayne is sipping brandy in the parlor of the B&B with insufferable birders who drone on about elegant trogons and yellow rumped swallows until you want to shout—"Duck l'Orange, anyone?"

You unfold the plot map on the bed and look at the ten acres of desert that belonged to your brother Eddie, a small craft pilot who never settled down. Who knows how he acquired the land? Dayne likes to say he won it playing Texas Holdem in Tombstone. But you know better. Eddie was never lucky at cards. After the accident, you learned he'd left the land to you.

The next morning you convince Dayne to skip the B&B's gourmet breakfast, much to the amazement of Lawrence, a tall birder from Minnetonka, who is orating on the migratory habits of humming birds over bacon and eggs soufflé.

"Man, that bacon smelled great," says Dayne wistfully, as he starts up the rented Pathfinder.

You raise an eyebrow. "How can you even dream of eating anything with a face on it, amidst a gaggle of precious birders?"

"I didn't see any face on that bacon, Kat, did you?"

"We'll have an early lunch in Bisbee," you say. "I just wanna get out to the land before I lose my nerve."

The two of you drive in silence through the brown, dry desert. It's February and the mesquite trees are bare with blackened bark. A hawk soars over the high desert plain, escorted by a threesome. He doesn't seem too bothered by the smaller dive-bombing birds, though you figure enough of them could knock him out of the sky. Hey, who needs a bird sanctuary?

"What?" says Dayne, as if he read your mind. Sometimes he's psychic, but doesn't know it.

"Who needs a spendy bird sanctuary when you can see all these birds here for free?"

Dayne chuckles. "For the gourmet breakfast and afternoon pie, of course."

You both share a moment—those were the winning particulars on the B&B's web site that sealed the deal.

"So, we must be getting close," says Dayne, scanning the desert.

You look at the plot map sent by a realtor last year. It's Valentine's Day, the anniversary of Eddie's death and you have chosen this day to see what he left behind. It hasn't been easy. The crash was sudden. Poof—gone—no chance to say goodbye.

"What mile marker are we looking for?" asks Dayne.

"Forty three. Isn't that weird? That's how old he was when he died."

"All right, don't go zen on me, Kat. Damn, I wish this truck had GPS."

Dayne's a gadget guy.

"All right," you say, "lets see what's coming up… looks like 33, without my glasses. So, we're probably ten miles away."

But you drive for another twenty without seeing any more markers. Finally a sign says: **Douglas 5 mi**.

"Shit," says Dayne. "Wasn't it supposed to be closer to Bisbee? I need a low-fat mocha in the worst way. Let's just go into Douglas."

"I don't want to go to Douglas."

"Well, if we keep driving we'll end up in Mexico, and I think AVIS will have a little problem with that."

"Let's turn around and backtrack. If we don't find it, I'll drop you off at Starbucks in Bisbee and come back myself."

You've come all the way from Seattle to see this land for the first time. You don't know what you expect to find. Maybe gold. Maybe a meth lab. Maybe an oasis in the desert for northwest gals like you in need of a little sun. Maybe some sign of him, something to hold onto.

Dayne pulls over beside a speed limit sign that says, **75 m.p.h.** You haven't seen another car for miles. "Do you really think they have a Starbucks in Bisbee?"

"Let's forget the whole thing," you say. "Let's go back to the B&B for fuck's sake and listen to Lawrence lecture on humming birds, okay? I mean, I've always wanted to know—do humming birds actually hum, or do they just sing in a language we don't understand? He'll know. And if he doesn't he'll make some shit up. What's the big diff?"

Dayne presses his lips together. Gazes at the horizon. Taps on the dash.

"Let's drive into Douglas," he says. "We'll get some gas, use the bathroom, and then head back. Wanna neck rub, later?"

You stare hard at the bleak terrain. Dayne turns on his blinker, which seems a ridiculous gesture on the empty highway, and puts the Pathfinder back on the road.

A roadrunner darts out from a tumbleweed and speeds across the pavement just in front of you, as if playing chicken. You see marker **42**.

"Dayne, did you see that?"

He grimaces. "Yeah, I saw it. But it doesn't necessarily mean anything. Who knows if there is a **43**?"

You pass a rusted tin building with a half-fenced in corral and vaguely recall some mention of an old building by the realtor, whose name you can't remember.

"There it is," you shout. "Marker **43**."

Dayne pumps the brakes and squints. "Damn, I'm starved. I wish we'd had the damn breakfast. Wish you had packed something."

"Turn right here," you say. "Right."

"I know," says Dayne. "I'm not stupid. I see **43**."

He drives the rental a little too fast down the teeth-jarring washboard road, his face set in grim determination.

"Jesus, look at these ruts," he says. "Must've been made by an awful big truck. They're like canyons."

A barbed wire fence runs along both sides of the road with hand written signs that say:

NO TRESSPASSING
DEAD EN

"According to the plot map, Eddie's land is on the other side of this parcel. There must be an easement," you say, "some kind of access or way to get there."

"Oh, don't go jumping to conclusions, now," says Dayne. "I wouldn't be too sure of anything out here, including that map. Including the assumption that anything will make sense."

"Gee, Darling, thanks for your support."

"I get grumpy without my espresso and power bar in the morning," he says, only half joking.

You spot a trailer all by itself among the high yellow grass.

"Stop the car. Maybe they'll let me walk across their property."

Wind blows dust across the windshield, rocking the SUV. "God, I feel like I'm in a Sam Shepard movie. Want me to go with you?" says Dayne, unconvincingly.

"No."

You get out and close the car door.

The trailer is dinky—an old Silver Streak with flat tires. A skinny, feral looking kid stands near a rusted swing set, but disappears when he sees you. Cold wind knifes through your Patagonia parka and you stand there, frozen.

No one comes out of the trailer. You don't move for the longest time. You gaze south across the barren land towards distant mountains and feel an immense sadness. Nothing but mesquite and cactus and yellow grass waving in the wind. Wind roars in your ears. It sounds like a great river or perhaps a truck moving down the highway. Or a Piper taking off.

You turn around and climb back into the Pathfinder. Dayne's embrace envelopes you.

You are grateful for his lasting hug.

For the warmth of the cab.

For his handkerchief offering.

But there are no tears. Only a heaviness inside you. You look at your husband and smile a little smile with all you've got. "Feel like some pie?"

Dayne navigates slowly, carefully back to the highway, then picks up speed and drives towards Bisbee. An enormous black vulture brazenly feeds on a flattened, furry carcass in the middle of the road. As the Pathfinder gets closer, the vulture doesn't move. Dayne bears down on it. You watch, mouth open.

The savvy desert bird is hungry but not stupid. At the last second, she lets go of her carrion and lifts off with tremendous wings, flying out of harm's way, an entrail trailing from her beak.

Resume for a Guru

I'm applying for the job of guru you advertised for on Craig's List. I feel qualified for the job. My name is Barbed Wire, barbed wire having been the first thing my mother saw upon opening her eyes following my birth under the bushes on the dairy farm. I live up to my name—thin, strong, intermittently sharp. Few cross me. Barbs speak louder than words. Enormous mammals in fact keep their distance. Few dare attempt to trespass or escape. I'm a keeper of herds. A catcher of roving tumbleweeds. Artists make ironic statements with my strands. I lead a simple life. Am light on this earth. Solid posts are my only attachments. You see me along the road, atop a fence, on ranches and prisons, galvanized and strong, classic and secure, capable of containing man, beast, & belief.

Disappearing Act

I take up magic tricks because I like the thrill of surprise and because you never know, in today's economy, magic just might come in handy. I start with cards and kerchiefs and work my way up to pulling rabbits out of hats. I'm stoked! But it turns out, rabbits don't want to go back inside the hat—and who can blame them. Soon my place is filled with the softest, sweetest little creatures you could ever meet.

I give them names like Big Ears and Bugs and Peter and Flopsy and Mopsy and Cottontail, and of course Lucky, but I can't keep up with the names and it comes down to the magic tricks or my bunnies. In the end, I go with plan B and stick with my bunnies, and keep it to a few card tricks on the side.

One day my daughter graduates from high school. A golden time. Her happiness lights up the room. She thinks my bunnies are adorable, and of course I fall in love with her all over again, my baby daughter now a young adult. I ask what her plan is—she answers: *vroom vroom*.

In the driveway sits a gleaming motorcycle.

Every parent wants better for their child than they had for themselves. At eighteen I dreamed of riding across country just like Easy Rider, flipping everybody off—with a double bird as my own personal touch.

Darling, wear your helmet, I say, and fly with care. Adventure changes your life.

She smiles shyly. I follow her gaze to a young woman her age in white leathers next to the bike. Skinny, young and awkward. I wonder how they will make it—how is that even possible? My parents must've thought the same when I volunteered to teach in a jungle during a war, me thinking, yeah, I can deal.

My Bella graces me with a long warm hug. She kisses my cheek and walks out the door. Through the window I watch her companion climb on back. Bella guns the throttle, waves a purple glove, and rides away… one last disappearing act.

Night Owl

Carmen sleeps until one in the afternoon and eats breakfast for dinner at 4:00. When her neighbor Cleve arrives home from his work, she's just getting started with hers. He hears her moving around in the flat upstairs, a ball rolling across the wooden floor, followed by the cat in pursuit, then her voice. Carmen hums as she paints and in the sounds she makes he sees color. He coughs. She stops. They listen to the sounds of evening— frogs in the pond, a distant bird of prey. He smokes and stays up way too late for his delivery job that starts at dawn.

The cat finds something, a pipe cleaner. Another life and death struggle ensues. And when the cat pounces and pauses, the pipe cleaner gripped in its paws, Carmen resumes her humming and Cleve falls asleep, metallic purple pulsing in his mind.

She paints through the night, the cat fast asleep, Cleve lightly snoring downstairs—inspiring strokes of yellow against the purple canvas of the night. Her upstairs light casts a small glow on the ground below, where his pickup waits for morning.

Pink Fleece

He glimpsed the pink of her fleece coat through the trees from the porch of his cabin, a moving flash against brown trunks, green boughs, and grey sky. Who wore pink in the woods? A City Girl. Was she here with her boyfriend?

Luke returned to the postcard he was writing to Mary Beth.

Dear Sweetheart, it began.

It's what came out of his pen. But his eye told him it didn't feel right. Now it was on the Camp Emandal postcard he'd paid two dollars for with a watercolor of a deer drinking down by the river and he thought, too late—it's in ink. Kind of like the relationship. Damn metaphor. Damn ink. Damn pink fleece.

Truth was they'd glued things back together with weekly $150 sessions. No cracks showed. But would it hold water? That's what he wanted to know.

That's what the therapist would not tell him.

The psychic on the other hand advised him in no uncertain terms he should appreciate what he had, not what he didn't have, that he needed to vacuum out his mind and stop thinking. Right. He liked her over the phone, a cat lady somewhere in Canada. But then she retired. How did a psychic retire? Could you turn off the visions?

One night at Smitty's, his pal Dodge went straight to the heart of the matter. "Luke, I've had a beer and I'll tell you the truth. You are your own worst enemy."

That brilliant analysis only cost him a Pliny the Elder. Well, two.

Luke went inside the cabin and filled a glass with mountain spring water from the tap. Took a sip. Walked down to camp. He played ping pong with friendly strangers, attempted yoga with Leo the rough and tumble water color instructor, tried to make a potholder out of fabric, decided to call it a welcome mat for one foot instead.

Saw no pink fleece in camp.

At twilight he walked to the river. A pink sunset reflected in the fast moving water. A doe appeared, eyed him tentatively, and took a sip.

Bathrobe, Biscotti, & Bike

Truman watched from the kitchen window as Fiona walked to the bus stop carrying her billboard briefcase, which included the lunch he'd made for her.

He hummed along with Mozart as he rinsed the breadboard, did a little tai chi as he put away the bread, the jelly, and the extra chunky peanut butter.

Something caught his eye.

He bent down to the checkered linoleum and peered closely. It was the chocolate dipped biscotti, individually wrapped, that he'd tucked into her bag as a surprise. It must've fallen out when she re-packed her billboard briefcase.

He picked it up and brought it close to his nose. Such a perfect treat. "Your safety," he said feeling ravenous, "cannot be guaranteed."

Truman ran outside, forgetting he was still in his robe, but instantly aware he was barefoot by the cold slab of concrete. Fiona's bus pulled away. He hopped on the bike of his 8-year-old neighbor Sam and began pedaling. The bus had one more stop before the freeway. With a bit of good fortune—perhaps a commuter with inexact change, he just might catch it.

For he was no ordinary stay at home retired house spouse in a robe, Kleenex in his pockets—he was Bathrobe Man with a job to do. Gripping the individually wrapped biscotti firmly between his teeth, Truman held on to the handlebars with both hands and pedaled hard, bathrobe belt blowing in the wind behind him.

Jarrod's Toes

"It's a little early in the morning for that, don't you think," says Jarrod, swigging his Miller Genuine Draft.

I shrug. "Must be noon somewhere in the world. I'm just gonna try it."

We're sitting on our redwood deck watching the dawn of a new century break over the East Bay hills. The sky is pink and orange and a deep, cool blue. I'm wearing my robe and bunny slippers; Jarrod's wearing sweats and is barefoot.

We're early risers. The kind of disciplined addicts who always stay high. Each night we say our prayers and pop our Valium. At 3:00 a.m. we wake and smoke a joint. By 6:00 we're drinking beer before the Valium and pot wear off.

"You don't have to do this to yourself," says Jarrod. "I don't know what you're trying to prove."

"I'm not trying to prove anything," I say. "I just wanna try this sober thing out, you know, for the brave new millennium."

Jarrod puts his long feet up on the deck railing and leans way back in his chair.

"Okay," he says. "All I ask is that you don't hide it, okay? If there's anything I can't stand it's a sneak."

"I don't plan on hiding it, Jarrod. What's the big deal? It's just a little experiment. You're not against experimenting, are you?"

"Did I say I was against experimenting? There's something to be said for the tried and true, just sayin'. But it's your life—do what you want. No skin off my teeth."

I look to see if he's smiling. He's not. "Look, if you don't want me to try this just say so. I won't do it. I won't do it if you don't want me to."

Jarrod rolls his stoner blue eyes. "And then you'll be resentful. And then I'll get to live with that for a while. No thanks. Why can't we keep things the way they are? This is the best show in town," he says, looking off towards the East Bay hills as if he's talking to them and not me.

The sun is over the ridge now and the sky has turned milky blue. It's been three hours since I've ingested any chemicals, a world record for me, and I figure I'm heading for dangerous waters.

Jarrod lights a joint of exceptional green bud. "Why do you have to experiment? That's what I'm trying to wrap my head around. And what will our friends think?"

"How will they know?"

"They'll know. You think you can hide that kind of thing? You'll be heading for the bathroom every time a bong is lit. You'll have to make a store-run when the blow and mirrors come out. You think they won't notice you nursing the same undrunk beer all night? They're card carrying potheads, babe, with a high Stoner's IQ living the wake and bake dream."

"Maybe you can help. Maybe you can drink half or something."

"Oh no. I'm not helping you out with this, Mona Lisa, baby. I love you but I won't be your co-dependent. I won't sit back and watch you ruin your life—our life—and all that we've built together."

The birds have begun to sing just a little too cheerfully in the oaks and bays around our house and my toes are starting to sweat inside the bunny slippers that Jarrod gave me last Christmas. I look at his narrow toes sticking above the deck railing. They seem to grow longer and longer, like ten peculiar shafts shooting up towards the sky.

"So you don't want me to do this?" I say to the side of his face.

"I didn't say that."

"But you won't support me? You won't at least help me try this sobriety thing?"

"Mona-L, I love you too much to stand idly by and watch you ruin your life, our life together."

"You said that already."

Jarrod looks at me. His eyes are red and filmy. In one hand is the joint, and in the other he's switched to coffee with brandy in search of that elusive chemical balance.

"Are you fucking with me," he says.

"No, I'm just pointing out that you repeated yourself."

"I know I repeated myself. We repeat ourselves everyday. It's called consistency, babe. Beautiful fucking consistency..."

His voice trails off. I hardly hear him. I'm watching his toes grow longer and longer, the most bizarre sight, and I think of Pinocchio's nose.

"You remember Pinocchio?"

"The porn place in the Barbary Coast?"

"No, the children's story."

There is silence. I can tell Jarrod's drawing a blank. Or maybe he's tuned me out. His eyes are closed; he sports a goofy grin. He tilts further back in his chair, way back, and I think he's going to fall backward until I see that his long toes have curled around the railing and are holding him prone, suspended in a stoned state of balance and bliss.

The morning sun is hot and way too bright and Jarrod's toes are just a little too vivid and I have this feeling that there's too much day in my eye. I tell myself everything's fine, it's just a little sobriety thing, a bit of turbulence that'll pass, like a bad trip. But once panic finds purchase, it's only a matter of time before that familiar craving takes over, a pull not unlike gravity. I reach for Jarrod's toes, and feeling them, I slowly come back to earth.

The Most Shoplifted Poet in America

"Would Bukowski be in poetry?" I ask the young man who is reading behind the counter. I'd already gone to the poetry section and perused the 'B's with no luck.

The young man smiles. "We keep Bukowski behind the counter here."

"Why is that?"

"He's the most shoplifted poet in America."

Once in a Venice Beach bookstore, I'd gone to the "B's" and found the same thing.

The clerk invited me behind the counter and I discovered a treasure trove of Bukowski titles I'd never seen. Above Bukowski was John Fante, also on the endangered list. Interesting because Fante was not well known, but Bukowski admired him, was a friend. Did that mean the book thieves were actually reading Bukowski and then Fante to see what Buk saw? Feel what he felt?

Who else? I wanted to know.

"Murakami," said the clerk.

"Hmmm... what about Carver?"

The clerk smiled. "No, Carver's safe."

"Well, wait till the Murakami shoplifters find out how much he liked Raymond Carver. Those books will fly off the shelves."

The clerk grinned. There was a time I had to stop reading Buk. A magazine editor had rejected a piece of mine and said I had to quit sleeping with Bukowski under my pillow. I doubt he ever stole a Bukowski. I doubt he ever stole anything.

I paid for a copy of Factotum, shook the young clerk's hand. He was a screenwriter, taking a couple of years off grad school at UCLA. MFA? Yeah.

Years ago I too had worked in a bookstore and was pleased to see young people still interested. It restored my faith, I told him. He smiled and turned to the register to make change.

Then I slipped a copy of *What We Talk About when We Talk About Love* into my large leather coat.

Ray deserved that.

Divorced Man Must Sell Bed

DIVORCED MAN MUST SELL BED
KINGSIZE
HANDMADE
MEXICAN BRASS
SACRIFICE—$1000.00

On the bottom of the flyer, six phone numbers curled up on detachable slips of paper. There had been no takers. Down one side someone had scrawled—*BAD KARMA!*

I needed a bed and didn't believe in superstition. I did, however, believe in a good deal. I took a number and gave the divorced man a call. On the phone he was surprisingly soft spoken and calm. Yes, he still had the bed. I imagined a shiny, noble frame of ornate brass shimmering in the morning sunlight. I didn't know what else to ask over the phone. What else can you ask about a bed? Is it hard? Is it soft? Has it ever been peed on? What about fleas? Was it the source of your marital problems? Does it come with pillows?

None of these questions came to my tongue. I asked to see it and he gave me the address. He lived on the beach near the Playa Java Café, where I'd seen the flyer. He was older than I imagined, though maybe not, for his face was still smooth except for deep lines gouged under his eyes. His hair was completely white.

He showed me to the master bedroom of his condo, a room that looked temporarily uninhabited, like a hotel room. Everything felt tidy, in order. There was an amazing absence of bric-a-brac. I scanned the dresser tops for a picture of his ex, but they were empty except for two red and white doilies.

The bed was a piece of art and immediately I knew I must have it. It was far less ornate than I'd imagined, yet its fluted lines of polished brass formed such an appealing and graceful keep that it was all I could do to suppress my excitement and therefore retain the upper hand in negotiations.

"Would you take six hundred for it?" I asked.

He chuckled. Not derisively, more the way a man might laugh to himself after reading something in the paper. He moved to the window, stared out at the garden with hanging fuchsias. His silence made me uncomfortable.

I waited. "Look, it may be worth more than that to you. It probably is. But six is all I have."

He remained silent, kept his eyes on the garden, appearing to consider my offer. It was easy to see he was sad. He seemed a nice enough man, and even now, sported a blazer and necktie. His tussled white hair made me think he was a professor. What had happened here?

"How long has it been on the market," I asked, trying a different approach.

"Two weeks and three days. No, four days," he said. Two weeks and four days."

"Any other calls?"

"No. You're the first caller. Perhaps I should thank you," he said, again chuckling to himself.

I tried to imagine what kind of woman would leave a guy like this. Probably a red head, younger and wild. Maybe a former student who grew bored with the older prof, bored with condo life in a Mexican bed.

"Can you tell me anything more about the bed?" I asked.

The Professor put his hands in his pocket and said, "I bought it for my wife in Tuxtla. We were on our honeymoon when she saw the bed in a shop window. She was crazy about Mexico. Crazy about anything Mexican."

I could see this beautiful red head dressed in white, already getting itchy feet on her luna de miel, spotting the bed in the craftsman's shop, insisting upon having it. Refusing to leave the country without it.

Then the professor surprised me by asking, "Are you married?"

"No." I felt my bargaining position slipping away. "Why do you ask?"

"Because before I sell you the bed, there is something you must know."

It occurred to me that the Professor had not been weighing the amount of my offer, but the offer itself. As if the finality of selling their Mexican bed was finally sinking in.

"Dolores said that the bed made her dream of Mexico. Whenever she slept in it she dreamed of the jungle and people dressed in white. She spoke Spanish and had many lovers." His voice was even and distant, without bitterness.

"Did you have those dreams, too?"

He shook his head.

"Well then, it was probably just her, just inside her head, you know." I paused, then casually inquired, "Were you ever in her dreams in Mexico?"

He glanced at me sharply. "If you want the bed, you may have it for eight hundred."

I knew I'd crossed a forbidden line, a line he'd have crossed himself if I had just let him talk. And it had cost me two hundred bucks. Sort of.

I wrote him a bad check, knowing a bed like this went for two grand on Union Street. But I figured I was doing him a favor. He had to get rid of that bed before his healing process could begin. After that he could start dating again, perhaps someone of his ilk, a tenure track prof from the science department.

When I got the bed home I set it up in the middle of my studio apartment. Light reflected off its brass frame and burned bright lines in the Victorian walls. I climbed in under the covers without sheets and immediately fell into a deep and heavy sleep—a gift inherited from my father, who could sleep anytime anywhere and wake up refreshed, even after a ten-minute nap.

Mine was no nap. I dreamed I was deep in the jungle under a canopy of sword ferns and pink bromeliads and high arching trees of a dense, dense green. I was in the brass bed on the jungle floor waiting for someone, impatient for someone to arrive. Then I saw them approaching, the Professor and his red haired wife. They wore white and held hands. The happy couple examined me, as if I were no more than a curiosity, a funny orchid in a tree. The Professor chuckled to himself. They shared a secret in Spanish and moved on. I shivered in the tropical heat.

When I awoke I called the Professor, feeling remorseful about the check. Of course I couldn't pay him, I'd have to return the bed. The phone rang and rang. I was about to hang up when a smokey female voice answered, "Hola, que tal."

I quickly hung up. That night I moved the bed out to the sidewalk and went back to sleeping on my futon.

Short Walk on a Long Pier

Floating in the shadows of the ferry where a famous master once zenned, lived a sippy monk on a tippy barge called The China Sea. Each morning he walked the planks with a satisfied shrug and untied koans of kelpy lines until noon.

At lunch he played chess with seagulls on a skiff, and when high tide arrived, he paddled to the *No Name* for beer and read Li Po until closing.

No books were written about him. No one came to his door. But his elegant wisdom glittered like sea glass on the ocean floor. Lifting a conch shell to his ear, he heard the whisper of the universe. Placing the shell to his lips, he answered its call.

Evan's Essence

I visited my friend Evan at the V.A., found him in bed, smiling, wearing baggy flannels. Asked how he was doing.

"Oh, fine," he said, like it was last year, or five years ago, or fifteen or twenty.

I poured him a glass of water, noticed his left hand was gone. We played checkers until he started yawning. I promised to return.

The next day he was still in flannels, but these were blue and red checked, soft and comfy—just like smilin' Ev, his big brown eyes even bigger behind thick glasses he now wore. His feet were gone, kept it to myself.

We played checkers, talked baseball. Would the Giants repeat as champs, this being an odd year? Superstitious like any old player, Ev shrugged, grinned his Cheshire grin and drifted off.

I couldn't get to the VA for three days. When I entered his room Evan smiled, gone from the chest down now, covers pulled up around his neck. We skipped checkers and baseball, he asked about the kids—typical Evan. He was doing this his way.

Didn't stop me from crying.

"Don't be sad, Kenny. You're seeing the best of me. There's no time to complain about Lincecum's curveball, or worry about who owes who money," which made me wonder whether I'd repaid him that 5 spot when we went to see *On Any Sunday* in 8th grade.

We talked motorcycles.

I reminded him how he'd had his helmet and gloves before he had his first bike.

Evan chuckled. "Always wanted to be ready."

Saturday evening his nurse Shangri-La nodded gently and showed me to his room. I stared at rumpled covers, saw his smile on the pillow below those glasses. His lips moved. I edged closer, wondering if he was confessing his love for Shangri-La or admitting that he'd finished my stool in wood shop, helping me graduate on time, or perhaps he was imparting a universal secret, being the most agile spiritual explorer I ever knew... and I believe he whispered, "Love's the current upon which we ride."

His smile faded. Evan vanished. And his essence filled the room.

The monitor flashed. Shangri-La threw back the curtains. Outside the wind blew. Slender palms bent back and forth as if waving goodbye. A shooting star arced a silver trail against the satin sky. Somewhere, a baby beckoned.

Shangri-La slipped away to complete her rounds.

Begonia

The begonia sat in a pot on a shelf above a row of books, growing towards the light from a window on the wall. Requiring little water and little care, the begonia longed to read the books, whose spines she could see as her stems hung vine-like towards the floor. She gazed at titles: *Earthshine, Heaven Is All Goodbyes,* and *Because I Wanted To Write You a Pop Song,* intrigued. And as she stared at the titles on the spines of the books she created her own stories. A writer sat in the corner of the room tapping away on a slim and silver machine. One day he slipped a new book in between the others and when she saw the title, *The Happy Begonia,* she opened her solitary bud and unfurled luminescent petals, reaching not towards the window now, but the writer in his chair across the room.

How To Properly Dispose of a Night

They say living in the desert can drive a man crazy. We bought a single-wide Detroit Silver Wing down in Coachella Valley as a getaway. I did the demo, electrical, dry wall. Jose did the painting and interior.

Neighbors liked what we did, took to us. On Fridays we'd leave the condo on the coast and head east on the I-10 for the trailer park all weekend. Another trailer came up for sale. Crime scene. Totally trashed. But up against a hill, good view. And cheap. Neighbors urged us to buy it. Told us an old dude had lived there, looked like everyone's shell shocked uncle. Nice. Kept to himself. But had lots of visitors. Quick stops. Sometimes women. One night pops were heard. Gunshots or firecrackers—who knew? Cops came, Uncle was dead. Which answered that question.

We hauled away trash and broken chairs, tore down walls. Found three syringes and a chess piece, a knight, behind the paneling. No money or drugs. Jose works in a hospital and knew what to do with syringes. You don't just throw that stuff in the trash. The way you don't throw trash into recycle, or recycle into compost. Modern consciousness. Common sense. But what to do with the knight we found in the wall? What did Uncle have up his sleeve besides track marks? What windmills was he chasing out there between the cactus and mesquite?

We grabbed a shovel and walked out into the desert at sunset. Purple light colored distant peaks. We burned sage and watched as smoke rose to the place where knights and maybe all things go when walls have been torn down. Said goodnight to the chess piece properly.

Jose opened cold Modelos. We drank quietly, packed out our bottles, and properly disposed of them in the trailer park's recycle can. Venus twinkled in the western sky. We went inside and played Scrabble until one of us, maybe me, spelled Uncle.

A Story of No Consequence

Eli lived in a tiny house on wheels in the middle of an apple orchard. From May until October he slept outside in a swinging hammock beneath a large Golden Delicious. On those nights, the orchard was his room, the starry sky his ceiling, and though he had little money, and his house seemed like a closet to most, Eli felt like a fortunate man. The cool air was heavy and sweet with fruit. His landlord's wife opened her window and played cello in the parlor. Eli closed his eyes and followed her lilting music all the way to dreamland. Upstairs, his landlord wrote important legal briefs.

A cat appeared. Black and white and scrawny, with huge green eyes. He gave her food and named her Ana, short for Manzana. She followed Eli on his garden rounds. If he ignored her, she walked in front of his feet as if to trip him. He developed a looping roundhouse step and chuckled at the deliciously inefficient way to walk. Ana would wait for his foot to come around and spring for it with both paws. Eli would scoop her up with one hand and cradle her to his chest.

Every Thursday, he walked to the library. He owned no books. He had no room to store them, no reason to keep them on a shelf like a trophy. Everything he had, he used or loved and returned.

And that is the way it was with Ana when fall gave way to winter. Eli moved back inside. The landlord's wife closed the window while the landlord wrote important legal briefs upstairs. One evening Ana slipped away. Eli called her and filled her bowl but she did not return. All winter he worked in his high boots, pruning and stacking wood. When it rained he stayed inside and smiled at the memory of those looping steps, at her purr that had permeated his flannel. When the sun went down, he slept in his loft and dreamed.

In April, white blossoms appeared on the tips of sturdy branches. The landlord's wife opened her window and played to a silent orchard, while the landlord wrote important legal briefs upstairs. Eli and his tiny house disappeared, leaving light wheel tracks behind.

Guy Biederman's prose and poetry have been widely published in literary journals including *Blue Five Notebook, Medusa's Laugh Press, 2Elizabeths* and *Exposition Review*, where he was twice a winner in their Flash 405 contest. Third Wednesday published his story "The Most Shoplifted Poet in America" in print as flash fiction and on their blog as Poem of The Week. He's the author of two collections, *Parts & Labor* and *House Samurai*.

Guy has worked as a bookstore clerk, gardener, sports writer, publisher, and creative writing college instructor. He began writing in earnest as a Peace Corps volunteer during a civil war in Guatemala and used his work to cover the gaps in the walls of the goat herder's shack he called home.

Guy received an M.A. from San Francisco State where his teaching career began. For twelve years he published the literary magazine *Bust Out Stories*, as well as seven titles by local authors. Guy and his wife live on a houseboat with two salty cats in Sausalito, California.

www.ingramcontent.com/pod-product-compliance
Lightning Source LLC
Chambersburg PA
CBHW052014240626
47153CB00008B/2878